AJEEMAH
AND HIS SON

AJEEMAH
AND HIS SON

by James Berry

Willa Perlman Books

HarperTrophy®
A Division of HarperCollinsPublishers

Library of Congress Cataloging-in-Publication Data
Berry, James.
    Ajeemah and his son / James Berry.
        p.   cm.
    "Willa Perlman Books."
    Summary: A father and his eighteen-year-old son are each affected
differently by their experiences as slaves in Jamaica in the early nineteenth
century.
    ISBN 0-06-021043-5. — ISBN 0-06-021044-3 (lib. bdg.)
    ISBN 0-06-440523-0 (pbk.)
    [1. Slavery—Jamaica—Fiction.   2. Fathers and sons—Fiction.
3. Jamaica—Fiction.]   I. Title.
PZ7.B46173Aj   1992   92-6615
[Fic]—dc20   CIP
                                                        AC

Also by James Berry

The Future-Telling Lady

A Thief in the Village and Other Stories

Spiderman Anancy

When I Dance: Poems

For my father,
called Cousin Oldmaster

AJEEMAH
AND HIS SON

That wiping out of Atu and Sisi's wedding was always going to be one of the painful happenings.

It was the year 1807. The Slave Trade was on. By way of that trade, with all its distress, Africans were becoming Caribbean people and Americans. But the sale of Africans as slaves would end. In just another year or so a new British law would stop the British slave trade, and the Americans would soon follow. It would stop Africans being sold to be slaves on plantations in America and the Caribbean.

It was only the importing that would end, not slavery itself, nor the selling of slaves by their existing owners. Stopping the importing was a beginning, and a very welcome start to the end of slavery altogether. Yet even that beginning stirred up wild rage, resistance and awful reactions.

The new law soon to be enforced made people

who benefited from the trade all angry, anxious and bitter. The new law made plantation owners cry out. It made them furious at the idea of an end to their regular supply of a free labor force. It caused panic among the ship-owning slave traders and the local African dealers. All ground their teeth in fury and rage at the coming end of their money-making from selling slaves. And the slave traders became determined to work with new vigor. They became determined to beat that end-of-slave-trade dead-line, when no more slaves could be shipped; they would get and supply as many more slaves as they could in the short time left.

Remember here too that young people and chil-dren came into the slave treatment all the time. They too had to endure a life of no freedom for their parents and for themselves. All was personal for them. The teenage couple Atu and Sisi came into it. They were going to have to face their wed-ding plans ruined—gone, wiped away as dust.

Truly, European slave buyers would buy. Truly, African traders would obtain their prisoners for sale into slavery. They would find them, even if they had to make their own riots and wars to get prisoners to sell. The slave-trader groups geared and equipped themselves. Their surprise attacks became more unstoppable in the villages. Yet, with all that hidden trouble about, people simply had to go on living their lives.

It was the sunniest of afternoons now. Bird singing filled the day. All unconcerned, Ajeemah and his son Atu walked along their village road in a happy mood. The eighteen-year-old Atu was soon to marry. He and his father were taking a dowry of gold to his expected wife's parents. Going along, not talking, Ajeemah and Atu walked past groups of huts surrounded by bare ground with domestic animals and children playing. They passed fields of yam and grain growing robustly. Atu was thinking about getting married. He knew their coming marriage delighted and excited his sixteen-year-old bride-to-be, Sisi, as much as it did him.

"My father Ajeemah," Atu said, "isn't it really something that two other fellows—two others—also wanted to be Sisi's husband?"

Ajeemah didn't look at his son, but a faint smile

showed he was amused. "This bride-gift of gold I carry," he said, "will make Sisi's parents receive you well, as a worthy son."

"I thank you, my father Ajeemah. I know it's your good fatherhood and good heart that make it possible."

"More than my good heart, it's my thrift. My thrift! You know I'm good at not losing, but keep adding to our wealth."

"I know, my father, I know. I should have said, may you continue to have all blessings."

"And you, my son Atu. May you continue to have all blessings."

"Thank you, my father Ajeemah."

"Your mother smiles to herself when she thinks of your coming union with smooth-skinned and bright-eyed Sisi! Good singer, good dancer, that Sunday-born Sisi! Delights everybody!"

"Plays instruments, too."

"Oh, yes, yes."

His eyes shining, Atu said, "She's the best. She pleases everyone."

"Pleases everyone," the father agreed.

"And two other fellows shan't get her."

The father smiled, repeating, "And two other fellows shan't get her."

"I'm happy your first wife my mother is happy."

"Your mother is happy because you'll begin to live your manhood. And she waits for new children you and Sisi will have."

"And I'm nervous."

"Nervous?"

"Yes. I'm nervous of all the preparations and ceremonies to get through."

"That's usual. Marriage makes even a warrior nervous. Especially first marriage."

"I'll try to enjoy being nervous."

"Wisdom, wisdom, from a young head!"

"Thank you, my father."

"Atu, when we get to the house of Sisi's father— Ahta the Twin—watch his face. Watch for the look on his face. First when he thinks I'm empty-handed. Then next when he sees me lift the two pieces of bride-gift gold, one from the inside of each sandal I wear."

Everybody knew Ajeemah worked in leather and

all kinds of skins. In the village he was called "Skin-man." He preserved animal, alligator and snake skins and made sandals, bags, belts, bracelets, knife sheaths, ornaments, talismans and pouches for magic charms and spells. But Ajeemah was also known for his practical jokes. He'd chuckled to himself, thinking up the way he'd present Atu's dowry in a most individual and unusual way. He'd created himself the special pair of leather-stringed, lace-up sandals with thick soles. Each sandal had a space under the insole to fit and hide the bride-gift gold in, while he walked to Sisi's house. Ajeemah's big joke was that he'd arrive as if empty-handed. Then, while talking, he'd simply take off each sandal, lift up the insole and produce his gift by surprise. But Atu wasn't at all sold on the idea.

"My father Ajeemah," Atu said, "suppose Sisi's father Ahta the Twin is displeased, and things go wrong?"

"True, my son Atu. If Ahta the Twin is displeased, that would be a disaster. But Ahta will not be displeased at all! With the sight of gold for him, Ahta's grin will split his face in two."

Atu laughed with his father. Won over, Atu now enjoyed his father's scheme along with him. Laughing together, they came around the corner of the footpath, between high bushy banks on each side of the track. And ambushed, with total surprise, Ajeemah and Atu were knocked to the ground, overpowered, by a gang of six Africans with two guns, two dogs, and knives and sticks. With lightning speed, three of their fellow Africans tied Ajeemah's arms behind his back, tightly bandaged his jaws—so he couldn't cry out—and shackled his legs with a chain. The other three tied and shackled Atu the same way. Then, to allow them to see and breathe but not identify, the kidnappers put a bag— a dirty, sickly stinking hood—right down over each captive's head and face.

The kidnappers stood now and stared at the older man. Ajeemah had on more than just a loincloth and his special sandals. Ajeemah wore his magic-spell amulet like a black leather armband. And he wore a flamboyant jacket made of the whole skin of an animal. The front of the jacket was held together with a stringed snakeskin lace; the sides were netted

with round and square holes; the back was length-
ened with tails of monkeys and lions all round. The
leader and his second-in-command both carried the
guns. They spoke both the other men's language
and Ajeemah's. The second-in-command said to
Ajeemah, "All dressed up, eh?"

The bushy-bearded leader had thick-set shoulders
and short, bulky thighs and arms; he walked with a
waddle. Admiring Ajeemah, he took a few steps
around him and answered, "Yeah. Looking like a
proper local prince."

"Ain't he just," the second-in-command said, un-
doing Ajeemah's jacket to take it off him. "This'll
do me very nicely!"

"Wait!" the bearded leader warned him. "Wait!
You better watch it!" And he and the others pointed
to the magic-spell amulet Ajeemah wore like an
armband. "Take one thing from them," the gang
leader went on, "and you begin to rot. Every day
you wake up a bit more rotten and deformed. A
hand falls off. Then another. A leg dries up. An eye
closes. Never again to mend. And you're driven
raging mad. Haunted, till you just go dumb. Not a

word ever again to come."

Horror, awe and dread blanketed the kidnappers' faces. The hand of the second-in-command fell from Ajeemah's jacket as if the words he heard paralyzed it. He commanded, "Get moving!"

Eaten up with rage, with everything in them saying, "Strike back!" Ajeemah and Atu stood their ground. Blows from a stick rained down on their backs with cutting pain.

"Hold your stick," the waddling leader said. "These two are real specials. There's a top price to be demanded for them. We mustn't damage these strong, good-looking bodies." He signaled the dogs. And growling with menace, the dogs leaped up and gripped the captives as if ready to butcher them till called off. Ajeemah and Atu obeyed and found themselves walking. And with their hands tied, their legs chained, from that moment Ajeemah and Atu would experience treatment they had never believed possible. The kidnappers took Ajeemah and Atu through a wood down to the river. A small boat waited at the bank of the river, guarded by two men with a gun. Four other men and two women were there, shackled and tied together, lying down in the boat.

Ajeemah and Atu had their hoods removed. Made to get into the boat too and lie down, they had their legs tied to the others'. The boat moved off. Ajeemah remembered his gold in a terrible fright, while his ankles were handled. At first he thought he might have lost the gold, then that his guard might have wanted to steal the sandals.

Ah! he said to himself. I still have it! I have Atu's bride-gift gold. I still have on my sandals! That's a good sign. This bride-gift is for my son's bride and goodwill for their children. For nobody else. Nobody else must ever get this gold. I must guard it. Always! . . .

The boat sailed and stopped several times. Sometimes it waited a long time till other captives were brought, Eventually the boat was full.

Night came down. Like all the others with them, Ajeemah and Atu were parched with thirst, empty with hunger and stifled with heat. They were weak. But they were taken from the boat, hands tied and ankles chained. They were made to walk a painful, killing distance in dim lantern light to their overnight stay in hard, bare, prisonlike barracks, where they were given tiny bits of food and very little to drink.

Next day they traveled early and arrived at the coast by dusk. They found themselves taken into a hot, airless, stinking old fort full of other captives. Well guarded, everybody was in some body pain or plain misery. With many hundreds there together, chained up sitting or lying on the floor, the place was a horror of groaning, crying, swearing and noisy gloom. Everybody was in terror over what was going to happen to them.

Next morning, after eating, Ajeemah and Atu found themselves going through the strange business of being oiled up to look clean and shiny for display for sale. In many ways they were lucky. Their trader had put them with a specially selected lot of youthful and strong-looking men, to attract the highest price.

Ajeemah was getting oiled by helpers when the bushy-bearded leader of the kidnappers waddled up, supervising.

"Hello, chiefman!" Ajeemah called. "Chiefman!"

He looked at Ajeemah. "What?"

"A word with you."

His gun hitched up on him, the bulky-limbed, bearded African came close and asked, "What you want?"

Ajeemah said, "Where am I going? What's going to happen to me?"

"Don't worry. You won't be eaten." The kidnapper slave trader said that because of a long-standing belief circulating among captives that white men bought them to eat them.

"Then tell me, how long will I be away?"

"It's up to your buyer to tell you that."

"I beg you, do a kind favor for me."

"What's that?"

"Do get a message to my women and children for me. Tell them Ajeemah—Ajeemah and Atu—say we'll be back soon. First chance! First chance we'll be back."

"Forget it. I don't even know where you come from."

"Remember where you got me and my son?

Remember? Ask. And get a message to Ahta the Twin—father of my son's bride-to-be. Tell Ahta—"

"Forget it, man. Forget it! I don't know where you come from."

"I'll tell you. Get a message and I return a good deed for you one day. I come from—"

"Listen. Most I can do for you is to get you in with the best captain I can. D'you hear me?" The slave trader began walking away.

Ajeemah was desperate. He shouted, "You must do something. You must! My four-year-old son, my son of birth pangs I shared, my Kufuo, must know I'm coming back. He must know!" The slave trader stood and watched his desperate captive. Ajeemah pleaded more quietly. "My little fellow must know something. No good-byes linger with us. No last tender feeling exchanged—to sustain us! Say you'll get a message—to my family. Please!"

The kidnapper despised Ajeemah for talking like that. He looked at Ajeemah as if he'd just disgraced himself shockingly. "You've looked like a prince," he said, "and behaved like a warrior, till now." He waddled away and went on with the supervising of his slaves being made ready for sale. And standing in groups, black faces, chests, arms and legs well oiled and shining, the people were put on show for the white captains of the waiting ships to come and choose their purchase.

Ajeemah and Atu had never seen a white man. They held in their tension and terror and watched the strange creatures. Ajeemah wondered if his flesh would end up in the flesh of one of the white men in captain's hat and high boots.

In a stream of captured people, Ajeemah and Atu were taken on board ship that same day. Other slave passengers were already there. By the end of the day the ship was full of sad, frightened, grief-stricken and wildly angry people chained up together. Over three hundred of them, they lay side by side on fittings like layers of shelves.

When the ship pulled away, noisy weeping and sobbing broke out. Screams of terror rose up and ripped through the decks and echoed back to land. And as the coast of Africa disappeared, a long-drawn-out groan of grief rose up together steadily from the people one after another, till all died away into silence.

Every African on board belonged to the captain. He had paid for them all. And they were his goods to resell at stupendous profit, way, way above purchase price. To keep costs down, and sail with as many slave people as possible, the captain's way would prove to be unprovoked punishment and frightening misery for his cargo passengers. But, for now, all were simply in a state of shock, felt as extreme bewilderment.

All a mixed-up lot—chained to the deck to heavy iron rings—the people were mostly strangers and enemy-tribe individuals at one another's side. Ajeemah and Atu were not together, and each didn't know where the other was. Atu called out, "My father Ajeemah? Are you here? My father—"

"Yes, my son Atu. I'm here!"

"My father?"

"Yes, my son."

"We've both fallen into hell!"

"Into jaws of monsters, my son!"

"Into jaws of monsters, my father! Into jaws of monsters!"

"Always—remember—always, there's a way out. There is a way!"

Neither father nor son said anything else. Each one began to think of his own terrible situation.

Ajeemah remembered the bride-gift gold. Again he'd forgotten it and was shaken with the dread he might have lost it. He moved his toes about—one foot and then the other. Ah! he said to himself. I still have on my sandals! I have Atu's bride-gift gold! Ajeemah thought how sometimes he'd forgotten the sandals for long stretches of time. But every time he could, he'd tightened up the strong leather-stringed sandals' laces. The bride-gift is safe is a good good sign! thought Ajeemah. A really good omen! I lost my jacket when I was oiled. I looked—and it wasn't there! Somebody took it. Just walked off with it. But—Atu's marriage gold is safe! . . .

Oh, how guns, dogs and mighty kingdoms smash up a man! Smash up his manhood and cut up his pride! They've scourged me and want to make me a disgrace. Oh, I won't let them. I won't let them. They want to take away my manhood and nationhood and add them to theirs. They want to take away all my days and nights and add them to theirs.

I won't let them. I won't let them. Kingdoms and individuals are bandits who attacked me and my son. They've reduced me. But they won't disgrace me any further. The good sign of Atu's bride-gift is with me. And I'm far from dead. Far from dead! Ajeemah opened his mouth to call out to Atu to tell him the sandals were intact and all right. But he changed his mind. I better not, he told himself. I must give away no hints whatsoever. Gold is gold! And it's Atu's marriage gold, for goodwill. Goodwill toward Atu and his children, from me, his father. So I must defend it, till—somehow—the right intention is done. All powers in me well know I will kill, or be killed, in defense of this gold! It is Atu's marriage gold!

While Ajeemah was there thinking about Atu's gold, Atu himself was thinking about the girl he planned to marry. . . . O Sunday-born Sisi! Sisi! What will become of our wedding day? You were to be my first wife. And here I am at sea chained up in pain, on a creaking ship, going where I do not know. . . . I must take everything about you with me. I must remember every detail of your face.

Take you in my head so you're with me. And you
keep my company. And your walk, your talk, your
gestures, your laughs and giggles, like your songs
and dances, all keep you in body with me. . . . And
Atu remembered how with friends and family people he and Sisi had entertained, danced and enjoyed
themselves in the evenings. As they danced and
sang, someone would put a favored person's name
into the song whether the person was present or
not. He would put in Sisi's name. And they danced
and sang:

> *Come here O*
> *Come let's play and dance osibi*
> *Come O Sisi*
> *Come here O come here*
> *Come let's play and dance osibi*
> *Come let's meet in moonlight*
> *Come here O Sisi*
> > *Sisi—come here . . .*

Then Sisi would put in his name:

> *. . . Come O Atu*
> *Come here O come here*

> *Come let's play and dance osibi*
> *Come let's meet in moonlight*
> *Come here O Atu*
> > *Atu—come here . . .*

On and on they would sing, with someone putting in a favored person's name.

Sisi was comical. Sisi could make everybody laugh. Sisi's elephant-act song came into Atu's head. Sisi became an elephant. Alone, the elephant hears drums playing. The elephant starts to dance to the sound of the drums. Sisi pushes a bulky shoulder, lifts a heavy foot, pushes a shoulder, lifting a heavy foot, nodding, pushing a shoulder, into a dance, all to the rhythm of the drum sound the elephant hears:

> *Dugu-dugu dugu-dugu-dom*
> *Dugu-dugu dugu-dugu-dom*
> *Dugu-dugu-dom, dugu-dugu-dom, dugu-*
> > *dugu-dom*
> *Dugu-dugu-dugu-dugu-dugu*
> *Dugu-dugu-dugu-dugu-dugu*
> > *Dugu-dugu-dom*
> > *Dugu-dugu . . .*

Unexpectedly, something popped into Atu's head like a spiteful explosion. Suppose one of the other two fellows should marry Sisi! . . . Suppose! . . . Suppose she didn't wait till he got back? . . . Would Sisi do that? Would she? . . . But then—Sisi wouldn't know whether he was in hell, in heaven or under the deep blue sea! She would have no idea where he was! Alarmed and anxious, Atu gave a loud sigh. He couldn't bear it. He couldn't think about it. But his new worry and Sisi's voice in her songs all became parts of the torture of his predicament. Sisi's voice was mixed in with the awful position he was in. Here he was—a chained-up young man in a ship at sea! Atu's eyes became filled with tears. The pain of his chained ankles, his bruising body, all began to tell him he was on a bitter journey. And all the time, bits of Sisi's singing floated in and out of his memory or circled around and around:

> *Dugu-dugu dugu-dugu-dom*
> *Dugu-dugu dugu-dugu-dom . . .*

> *Come here O*
> *Come let's play and dance osibi*

Come O Atu . . .
  Come O Sisi . . .
Come here O come here
Come let's play and dance osibi . . .
  Come let's meet in moonlight . . .

After three weeks at sea, Ajeemah had taken in some terrible new sights. And he had added to himself a whole new range of painful feelings. Having to watch fellow passengers bawled at and struck by white sailors was an offensive abuse that burned him up with rage every time. And forced into close living with people of enemy tribes was agony that hardly lessened. But having to travel, wretchedly chained in a fixed position, in a stinking hole of a place was hell itself. No wonder at all people vomited regularly and had unexpected bowel movements. No wonder a man and a woman suffocated in the filthy stink of the ship. It was the two meals a day in fresh air on deck that kept everybody alive. It was that tonic relief of fresh sea air that revived everybody. When would he be able to tell his family about all this? When? Ajeemah wondered.

Six weeks of sea travel and Ajeemah and Atu arrived in Jamaica. They got themselves off the ship, limping: all sore, stiff, weak, half dead. To stand on land again and get fresh air was like a cool river wash in sunlight. The ship had been a foul, stinking, stifling place. And the ship's rolling and rocking, with them chained up in their narrow spaces, had rubbed and bruised and stripped their skin raw. Four people all together had died and been thrown into the sea. Both Ajeemah and Atu had lost their magic-spell amulets and didn't even care. But that his stringed lace-up sandals were still there on his sad, heavy feet was a magic sign that kept a light of hope ever burning in Ajeemah.

Soon, Ajeemah and Atu were displayed separately with others for sale. And quicker than expected, gates were opened and they had the sun-reddened excited faces of the white-men planters down upon them like hungry wolves, looking for the fittest and best for their plantations. But, also unexpectedly, the father and son were about to face their most painful and bitter moment.

Atu saw his father leaving, being taken away by a

planter while he was held, already bought by another plantation owner. Led along, Ajeemah looked back, calling desperately, "Atu, my son Atu—freedom! Freedom! Or let us meet in the land of spirits!"

Two hours' ride from Kingston, in the back of the estate horse-drawn carriage with two other male slaves bought with him, and Ajeemah came to his big and busy New World sugar plantation. Nearly four hundred slaves lived and worked here.

Everybody stepped down from the carriage in the center of the estate work yard in a blaze of sunlight. The estate work yard buildings spread out like a little village. The huge windmill that powered the grinding of the sugarcane was near the millhouse where the cane was crushed and where its juice was taken and boiled into the wealth-making sugar, and also rum. Then in a close cluster there were the boiling house, curing house, distilling house and trash house. Ajeemah stared at the windmill; he'd never seen a windmill. He then glanced at the many workshop buildings, the animal houses and the overseer's and headmen's houses. And he could see, separated some good distance away, the huts—the slaves' quarters. On his other side, not too far away on high ground, Ajeemah saw the dominant white Great House; it stood on grounds of gardens and whitewashed trunks of palm trees and overlooked the estate's sealike acres of sugarcane fields with slaves at work.

A look of pride came over the face of the old slave coachman. Smiling and looking proud too, the estate owner said, "Look! You see how different everything is from Africa?" And the coachman translated.

The coachman had made himself understood. Ajeemah came from the country now known as Ghana, where many Jamaican slaves had come from. But Ajeemah was in no mood to respond. His face merely stayed serious and unmoved. Here he was, confused, with his body all sore, stiff, tired and painful. His family in Africa didn't know where he was. He and Atu each didn't know where the other was. And he'd been taken to this terrifying place. All the well-laid-out orderliness of the place truly gave him a dread. This was exactly the sort of place where tyrant kings imprisoned, ill-treated and

executed victims. Ajeemah's hurt made him deeply
solemn, deeply sad. His position of no hope was his
anger turned to silent sadness. His position of no
fight back allowed was itself the pain of a bitter, bitter trap. The journey had made it impossibly diffi-
cult for him to work out how to find his return to
Africa. He thought of his secret gold; it stirred
nothing—stirred no cheerfulness at all in him. But
Ajeemah knew, at the bottom of it all, he'd have to
find a way to get back to his family in Africa, or
he'd have to take some terrible revenge.

On that same afternoon he arrived, without lug-
gage, without money or friend, Ajeemah was taken
to work under Felix, in the saddlery.

Silent and sullen, Ajeemah was taken into the big
opened-up workroom, cluttered with new hides
and all sorts of pieces of leather. He would work on
harnesses and saddles, deal with leatherwork for the
draft mules and horses of estate wagons and car-
riages. In fact, he would work on the estate's general leatherwork needs.

Confusion suddenly swept over Ajeemah. He felt
totally lost. A rush of bewilderment had made his

mind go blank. For a brief moment Ajeemah didn't
know where he was at all. It was like walking into a
little dream and out again. He came back to his
senses full of leather smells. And he was seeing a
woman and three men standing staring at him. The
people talked to him and to each other, but he understood none of the language these black people
spoke. Then Felix, the older man who was in
charge, spoke to him in something of his own language. Felix spoke loudly in an awful talking-down
way. That too only added to Ajeemah's feeling of
the strange, the alien and all that separated him
off—the new African.

After work Ajeemah found he was housed with
Quaco-Sam and his wife and fourteen-year-old
daughter in their big hut. Quaco-Sam had been
picked out to supervise Ajeemah, a new man: that
meant to talk to him, tell him the worst of the facts,
watch him but encourage him to settle down and
become a good, hard-working slave. Quaco-Sam
understood Ajeemah's language. He had come
from Africa as a teenager. From hard everyday
sweating in the fields, Quaco-Sam had worked his

way up to become head boilerman and sometimes a field-gang head driver. Quaco-Sam drove the workers hard. He snooped and reported on fellow slaves. Quaco-Sam received special gifts of sugar and rum and an occasional pair of cast-off trousers from the estate owner.

On the second night after Ajeemah's arrival, in the darkness of early night, Quaco-Sam and his family sat with him outside at the door of their hut. And in two languages—one for Ajeemah and plantation English for his family—the tall, big and deep-voiced Quaco-Sam went on as if he enjoyed reeling off consequences of trouble on the estate. "All day long," he said, "everybody a-talk an' a-talk 'bout freedom! Freedom! An' me say, tell me, wha' you know 'bout freedom? Look 'pon them who turn runaways! They live in woods livin' freedom, livin' wild hog life! They always in rags. They always tired, hungry an' a-parch with thirst. An' always, the military at they heel a-keep them runnin'. An' when they get caught—me tell you—they get bring back. An' they get beaten like a chop-up meat. Me wahn freedom, yes. But this freedom! Freedom! A expensive thing! Me still a poor, poor man. . . ."

Quaco-Sam translated what he and his wife said into African language for Ajeemah. His wife Phibba explained that if you behaved well, you weren't flogged. "Work good," she said, "you get no beat'n'. Behave good, you get no beat'n'." And Phibba went on telling Ajeemah that when an older woman was a gang driver, she was in charge of the estate's five- to ten-year-old boys and girls. She would drive them to tend, feed and water estate pigs, goats, poultry and pigeons. She would make them clean out the stable, tidy up the grain house and food store, sweep up animal droppings and do general light work anywhere necessary. And she would drive them to tend estate gardens. That woman driver used only a light whip. Phibba herself was driver of a second field gang. Her gang had the big girls and boys and old men and women, and did most of the hoeing and weeding.

Sometimes she really had to lash somebody hard, Phibba said. "Work mus' get done! An' in time! If the work noh done, me—me—get the beat'n'! . . . Me glad glad," Phibba went on, "me daughter here not a fiel' han'. That she work as kitchen han' at Great House. Much, much better!"

"Go watch the 'Great Gang' at work in a field," Quaco-Sam said. "The bigges', stronges' man an' woman through sunrise to sundown, you a-watch the sweatin' mule gang at work. You watch them clear land, dig holes and plant seed cane, cut the ripe cane in crop time an' work millhouse—night an' day in crop time—you a-watch work without pay."

"Everybody 'pon estate here mus' work hard," Phibba pointed out with emphasis. "Everybody *mus'* work hard!"

"True. Everybody. Everybody. . . . An' understan', Ajeemah, this is a life whey you have no money; you go nowhere; you have nothin'; but you get used to it, a-search fo' you extra little piece a fish head. You get your portion of rough cloth fo' clothes; you get you once-a-week piece a meat or saltfish; you get you plot a land to grow you own food; you have nothin'; but you get used to it, a-search fo' you extra little piece a fish head. Understan' that. . . . "

In three weeks now, this would be the third time
the estate owner himself, Mr. Fairworthy, called in
at the saddlery to see how the new man Ajeemah
was getting on. Dismounting and hitching up his
horse, Mr. Fairworthy came in and said, "Felix,
how's your new man settling down?"

"Very promisin', Massa. Very promisin'!"

The estate owner turned around to Ajeemah. "A
good place here, Justin. A *good* place!" And Felix
translated.

Ajeemah looked the estate owner straight in
the eye and nodded with emphasis. "Ajeemah!
Ajeemah!"

"No, no!" Mr. Fairworthy said, "Justin! Justin!"
He pointed at him. "You are Justin. Your name is
now Justin!" Felix translated Mr. Fairworthy as he
talked.

Ajeemah sighed and looked away. On Ajeemah's
second day at the estate, Mrs. Fairworthy had come
to the saddlery with her husband and remarked,
"So, my dear, this is our saddlery African just in?"

"Ah!" he'd said. "My dear, you've just given me
an idea."

"What, my dear?"

"The name, 'Justin.' We shall call him Justin."

Mrs. Fairworthy had laughed with amusement. And it had been made known that the name of the new African at the saddlery was Justin. Ajeemah hated the name and rejected it; yet it would stick: The long-settled estate population preferred the name to the African one.

Still looking away now, Ajeemah said, "Massa," and Felix took up translating him. "I am unhappy here. I have a little son, and oh, it's such a pain not to have him! Tears come like rain in my heart. My family knows nothing of my whereabouts. And I am the pride of my family. Tears, worry and lament now fill my family's days and nights over my vanishing. My women and children plant and harvest food with me. My women and children help me with my proud work in skins. Now—I without my women and children and they without me—all of us are sad. I gave no consent to be here. I was not a prisoner taken at war. I broke no law. I did nothing wrong to be made your slave. Massa Fairworthy, sir, my request is that, at the end of my request now, you arrange that I begin to return to my people. I need my Kufuo. I need a way back to him!"

Taken aback, the Englishman's pink and sweaty face looked cross, as if confronted by insolence. Then his face relaxed, as if wanting to look compassionate as he said, "Perhaps, Justin, you don't really quite understand. I actually bought you. Paid for you. You're very important to me. You are both my cash in hand and my working cash. I bought you because I expected good business out of you. Meaning profit. Now, if you were to buy yourself back, I'd look back for your purchase price, plus profit I expected to make over your whole life. Do you see that? . . . You are in no position to bargain, are you?"

Ajeemah's thoughts went straight to his secret gold under the heavy stone step. With no trunk or a bag or anywhere in his room to keep anything, at first opportunity, Ajeemah had moved the thick, heavy stone step at the back door, dug a deep hole quickly, carefully hidden his gold and replaced the rock. I could use the gold! he thought now. Could use it to bargain for my freedom! Then he remembered—without knowing he had some gold, Quaco-Sam had warned him. A slave couldn't own things. Anything a slave managed to get belonged to the estate. The estate could claim it! Once they knew he had his gold, who'd stop them from taking it away? Nobody would. Nothing could stop them. . . .

In Ajeemah's continued silence Mr. Fairworthy went on, "Who knows, Justin. You may well be able to buy yourself free one day. But certainly not yet. . . ."

Ajeemah still looked at nobody. Mr. Fairworthy wondered what he was plotting. New Africans had a way of trying to run away! He said to Felix, "Explain to him, I say he'll get used to it here. He'll soon see life here is much, much better than Africa. Tell him, too, if he ever tries to run away, he'll walk straight into the jaws of terrible, terrible beasts. Runaways live the most wretched life. Always on the run in the hills and valleys of the great woods. Our military men are always hounding them. Needless to say, most often they're caught, brought back and have themselves peppered with flogging, in front of the whole estate. . . . Tell him, in time, before too long, he'll come to settle down and be well contented and happy."

The new African spoke unexpectedly. "Well, Massa, help me to be happy."

"I want to."

"Well, Massa, help me find my son Atu."

"Your son?"

"Yes. Atu. He journeyed with me, over the wide sea and the many moons. And I've lost him. You did not buy him with me."

"Felix, tell him, it's better—much, much better—to think of having other sons here—right here—in this estate." His words translated, he turned to go but stopped to add, "Felix, keep a strict eye on this new fellow. Watch him. But help him to settle."

"Yes, Massa," Felix said. "Yes, sir."

Ajeemah felt trapped. What a world he'd come to! This world kept him in a trap, so it could take everything! Everything!

Same day, at lunchtime, twenty miles away, unknown to Ajeemah, his son Atu also made a request like he had. With his field gang, eating his brought cooked lunch under a tree, he won the attention of his estate owner, who'd ridden by and stopped to listen to him. Atu came forward. The estate owner called someone to translate for him.

Atu said, "Massa, I was to be married, today! Sisi should have been my first wife and I her husband. And I am here, with pain in my heart for Sisi, my flashing-eyed singer and dancer. Massa, fix it in reverse that I journey back to Sisi. Once she sees me, she'll forgive me—forgive my silly absence without good-bye. Let me go back to Sisi, Massa!"

The estate owner looked surprised. He was a little moved and softened. "Native boy in love," he said, "but you must know this: There's no going back for you! But you *will* be all right. Plenty of girls on the estate here! Find yourself another. Pick one. Find one here!"

"Well, Massa—" Atu hesitated. He went on, "Help me find my father."

"Your father?"

"My father Ajeemah. Over the big sea and many

moons, we journeyed here together. You did not buy him with me. And I lost him. I lost him, Massa. Will you help me find him?"

"I cannot. You will not find him. Impossible! Remember this: You have a new life. A much better life than in Africa. Settle down to your new life. You'll see you like it." He looked up and waved his hand. "All these well-behaved people with you here—with happy smiling faces—all were once new like you. All were once new! Now—go back to lunch." And the estate owner rode away, to his lunch.

Atu was shattered. He stood. What a condemned life I've come into! What an imprisonment called "happy"! He was sweating but felt icy, as if his guts had vanished and left him empty.

In bed that night, Atu's head was all full of remembering Sisi. But some other harsh, acrid feelings stuck stubbornly around his memory. Today, at work in the field, he was lashed—second time now—for not keeping up with his gang. It was the month of June. All the estate had gone mad with seed-cane planting. And that streaked mark of the cowhide lash across his back was a bitter offensive pain.

I won't stand it, Atu said to himself. I will not put up with these hurts they call "estate life"! One day—one day—I shall be full and wild and free, seeking revenge! But those feelings cleared. Sisi came back into his thinking: This was a wonderful relief. So, pleased, Atu grinned.

In his own hard log bed at night, Ajeemah too would fall asleep thinking about the family and friends he'd been wrenched away from in Africa. But that night he faced a terror that seized him from time to time.

Lying on his back, palms of his hands under the back of his head, his eyes facing the ceiling while his dim lamp burned low, Ajeemah was seeing that though he lived, he didn't belong to himself, and didn't belong to the people he loved, and he'd done no wrong to anybody. The truth of his position as a slave gripped him with a chilling horror. It made him feel swallowed by a nasty horrific monster. He was now inside its belly, becoming the flesh

of the monster, little by little. What of his future?
What of his family? What of this pain and torture,
this captivity, giving his life to Mr. Fairworthy?

Ajeemah knew he would never save pennies—
years and years from the sale of his garden vegetables—to buy his freedom. That freedom was already his very own. He'd decided he would never
try to buy his freedom back, as a few people actually did. How then would he get out of his enslave-
ment? How?

In a contrary way, Ajeemah was not at all bitter
about his work itself. He'd given himself to his
leatherwork. He loved the joy of handling, shaping
and using skin. And his work in leather had im-
proved to a quality he would never have imagined.
Also, he quietly enjoyed picking up and learning his
plantation English from Felix and others. But his
sense of abuse churned him up whenever he was
made to go and work in the boiling house or the
wagon-making workshop. Then, always, he knew,
he must swallow the extra offense. He must cover
up the hammering of his wounds. And he knew
that to everybody, he appeared to be settling. For

him, everything he did in all this New World business attacked him as a person. Attacked him as a way of life! And he was expected to swallow it! But, as far as he was concerned, all was only temporary. Only temporary! He merely needed more time, to learn and to plan. He needed time to find good, reliable, committed connections.

The busy round of seasons kept on. It kept on whether it was the making and looking after estate equipment, planting, weeding or reaping sugarcane or boiling sugar. One demanding time followed another. With all this life of hustle and urgency going on, relaxing time between work and bedtime was short. But Ajeemah turned this little time into his sweet relief of the day. In this soft early darkness of night, alone, sitting on his log stool, his back against his wattled hut, Ajeemah kept in touch, remembering his family and home in Africa.

Sometimes, in the evening, Ajeemah would mourn the loss of his eight children and their two mothers. He would endure the pain of separation from his children, not able to see them, be with them, or hear anything about them, and they too not knowing anything about him. He would think of the children in order of their ages. He would make a sad groaning sound for everyone, beginning with the first child, a daughter, then Atu, right down to his youngest, Efia, his daughter two years old. Then he would come back to his four-year-old son, Kufuo, and grieve specially, on and on. Sometimes, he merely remembered time with Kufuo.

Last night, Ajeemah came straight to Kufuo. His feeling and imagination strong, Ajeemah saw Kufuo as if he were actually with him in their home in Africa. Grinning, he talked loudly in his African language. He said, "Man-child—who had me share your mother's birth pangs—have you another handful of red bird's feathers you collected up to give me, saying it's all in your day's work? Eh, little lion? You don't have another handful? Well—the first handful is there. In the calabash. Beside the pieces of snakeskin!" He imagined picking up Kufuo and tickling him and enjoying his child chuckles. He whispered to himself, "Oh, I remember the smell of your breath! I remember your little hand in my big hand!"

Tonight, Ajeemah remembered laughing at Kufuo. And Kufuo, not liking it, saying to him, "My father, you mustn't laugh at me. You mustn't laugh at me."

He laughed at Kufuo because he wore coils of wisps around his little arm, to imitate his father's amulet. "I only laugh," he said aloud, "because you amuse me. You amuse me because you're such a little man! Such a little man!" And Kufuo was pleased. And, as he often did, Ajeemah settled down, lost in remembered situations and conversations with his son; remembering spoiling him, teaching him to use a spear; remembering them together trapping birds; setting their trap, then hiding, waiting in the wood . . . remembering singing together and Kufuo's child voice out of tune; remembering . . .

Secretly, all the time, Ajeemah looked for somebody to link up breakaway plans with. Reliable connections had to be built! But getting to spot a rebellious, trustworthy soulmate proved to be a slow process. Mostly, slave people were crushed people; they lived to survive and not antagonize;

they crawled for little favors. Ajeemah knew he had
to be careful with whom he talked rebellion.

And so—the estate went on, showing no mercy.

Its furnaces the biggest, smoke kept rising up
from them toward both the daylight and the night
sky. The estate kept up the loudest and most urgent
combined noises on the tropical landscape. The estate workshops contrasted clangings and hammer-
ings, wood sawings, animal voices and songs of
slaves working. In the vast lakelike fields of sugarcane, cowhide whips cracked on the backs of work
animals and black people washed in sweat. Wheels
of cane-laden wagons churned up their field tracks,
up to the work yard, where the sugar-making furnaces roared. And piled-up barrels of sugar, like the
piled-up casks of rum, were rolled out and taken
away to the wharves. And all this was the tune of
big profits. And all this happened with the enor-
mous group of seized people, robbed of their lives,
treated like work mules. All this permitted the master to be a kind of king, who accompanied his great
wealth to London regularly.

Ajeemah's secret plans began to speed up. Secretly he'd been seeing Kaleb, a field slave who'd been flogged out of bed to get up and go to work. Separately, he'd also been seeing Mercury, a freedman businessman, who had property and connections.

In the cover of darkness Ajeemah, Kaleb and Mercury slowly walked up and down the slavevillage road. They talked quietly.

"Estate wrong we bad bad," Ajeemah said.

"Estate block up a man own life way," Kaleb said, "an' batter him half dead."

"An' estate get away with it," Mercury said.

"Nobody—nobody—to stop estate wronging me," Kaleb said.

"Estate suck life out every slave man, every slave woman, every slave child," Ajeemah said.

"Half estate belong to slave people," Mercury said.

"More than half estate a-for slave people," Ajeemah said.

"An' them will never get it," Kaleb said.

"Get it?" Mercury said. "Get it? Fair deal fo' slave? Fair deal fo' slave? Never. Considering fair deal fo' slave would be miracle! Miracle!"

"So we make own court," Ajeemah said. "We make own court. We put estate on trial."

"Exactly!" Mercury said. "How else? How else will fairness happen?"

"We mus' make fairness happen," Ajeemah said, and his voice became deeper and low. "We mus' pass sentence on estate. An' make sentence happen."

"I tell you," Mercury said. "Listen." And he explained: At ten years old—forty years ago—he was tricked away from his parents in Africa and brought to this estate. To this day his parents couldn't have had one single word about him. He certainly had heard nothing from them. And thirty years he spent in slavery. Thirty years! And saving "one-one" pennies for twenty years, he bought his freedom, ten years ago. More excited, well worked up now, Mercury let his hands gesture strongly in the darkness. "Listen, man! I tell you. Understan'. I have black friends an' white friends, clean friends an' dirty friends, big friends an' little friends, law friends an' bush-rebel friends, country friends an' town friends. An' all—every one—believe in freedom! Every one wahn slaves free! Every one! Understan' me? Understan'?"

Ajeemah and Kaleb gave long and deep groaning sighs.

Ajeemah said, "I wohn pay fo' freedom. Never! Already that freedom mine when I born. Mine! Me freedom get robbed. I dohn pay fo' it back. Me dohn pay robber."

"Well," Mercury said, "I paid fo' my freedom back. With twenty years of saving pennies from vegetables I sell from my food garden I paid. I paid the Englishman for my freedom he said he owned."

"I wohn pay," Ajeemah said. "Me freedom a-for me! Fo' me own self. I get kidnapped. I get seized. Me life is robbed. Me whole life robbed from me. No. I dohn pay fo' it back. I pay no robber. I fight him. Me fight the robber. Fight him!"

The men walked along in silence for a little while, there on the slave-village road, in the darkness. They turned around and walked back again. How loyal and true was Kaleb? Ajeemah had a little doubt about that. He asked him, "So Kaleb, you really full-full decided?"

"Me?"

"You really wahn come in on the plan with me? An' have a job to do?"

"Come in on the plan?"

"You really really wahn to?"

"You know right now me in pain. Me back raw like a slice meat. Me skin cut up with beat'n'. Gimme the chance, an' you think me wohn pepper estate people backside too? That me wohn pepper they backside? Gimme poison, gimme the way, me poison the lot tomorrow. Massa first! That damn Massa first!"

"Good," Ajeemah said. "But Kaleb, you'll have a gun, not poison."

"Man, gunfire a quick-quick poison! You say gun dohn make quick poison cut-up? Me say, gun got best rotten-up fo' that Massa belly."

Mercury said, "Listen! I miself dohn wahn know what you wahn the guns fo' at all. You give me order fo' twelve guns, twelve horses an' ten rebel fighters, fine! I will supply all that. All made ready an' left somewhere agreed. Guns all nice an' neat in sugar bags. But, understan', my job's only delivery of order. An', of course, collecting my money from you fo' miself, fo' everybody an' everything. Agree?"

"Agree!" Ajeemah said. And a decision was reached. This stage of the plan was settled. Mercury would get in touch with Ajeemah again in ten days' time. He would let him know when, where and how to collect all items he ordered.

Ajeemah walked alone in the darkness back to his hut. And, as if he had a fever he had longed and longed for, Ajeemah's excitement roasted him. Things were moving fast now! He told himself: Now I can use my gold! Perhaps this is what my gold was meant for. Half my gold will go to pay Mercury. Go to pay for freeing myself! Freeing myself! Oh, Atu, your bride-gift may yet pay for us to meet again! Oh, Atu my son! Oh Atu! But how? How will it happen? How will the plan work? Oh, Atu, I'm going to make drama and confusion and pain for the cruel, cruel ways that rob us, damage us, and keep us trapped!

Ajeemah began thinking about that part of the

plan he'd told nobody about. That was the setting of the whole estate on fire at night. Set everything important ablaze. Get the millhouse, the boiler house, the curing house, other work-yard buildings, the Great House and the six biggest cane fields, all roaring together, in a glorious all-around upsurge of flames and smoke.

On a moonlit night, six rebel fighters on horseback would set the six biggest young cane fields alight. Swift on horseback, the rebels would set each field alight at its center and four sides. He, Ajeemah, and Kaleb would set the work-yard houses on fire at the same time with the cane fields. The other four rebel fighters would hide in wait around the Great House. When the flames of the cane fields and work-yard buildings lit up the sky, and Massa and everybody had left, rushed out and away, to stop fires, the Great House itself would be set alight. Then the rebel fighters would guard it till it was burned down to metal, concrete and ashes.

Ajeemah saw it that he and Kaleb would start, hasten and defend the burning down of the work yard. They would shoot all who tried to stop the fires. He would let Kaleb get away and free himself. He would stay and shoot it out with Massa and staff and the militiamen when they arrived. Unexpectedly, Ajeemah saw he would be shot and killed. He roared, "My son Atu, we promised! Let we meet in the land of the spirits! Let we meet up! In the name of freedom, let we meet up!"

Lying on his back in bed, Ajeemah whispered in his African language to his youngest son, "Hahah, Kufuo man-child, what muscles! So big big! When did your muscles get so big! I'll have to do something about mine. To stop your muscles getting bigger than mine, I'll have to rub my muscles with special herbs and oils!" And he imagined hearing his little son's tickled laughter. And he himself chuckled. And he began remembering Kufuo's voice, singing with everybody. And with sad feelings, suddenly, Ajeemah remembered—Kufuo would be older now: five years older. And he remembered too, five years now, he'd lived in Jamaica!

For three days after seeing Mercury, Ajeemah

lived in a wonderful dream world of the strong and the powerful. Seen at work, smelling of leather, tanning it, cutting it, sewing it, admiring it, Ajeemah gave no clues he felt ready to die. On the fourth day something dramatic happened.

The estate owner and a militia officer visited Ajeemah at the saddlery. They took him to the bookkeeper's house's back veranda. They made Ajeemah sit down while they too sat down on benches around him.

The tall, red-faced officer took a piece of torn brown paper from his redcoat pocket. He read the scrawled message:

MASSA STRANGA WAN COME BRIB
JUSTIN

His uniform spotless, his manner calm—all as if he didn't represent the law and punishment—the officer kept friendly eyes on Ajeemah. He spoke slowly. "This written message was dropped over the Great House gate while it was closed. Do you know who might send this message to Massa? With your name on it?"

Sitting there barefoot, in rough slave clothes, with face, chest and arms shiny with sweat, Ajeemah's black face was a blank. He shook his head. "No, sir. Me dohn know."

"Has anybody given you money—any money at all—or a gift, for a favor you have done? Or for anything you are doing, or selling, or planning to do for him or them?"

"No, sir. No!"

"Now, Justin, tell me. Who might want to tell something on you?"

"Me dohn know, sir." Ajeemah made himself sound very certain.

Mr. Fairworthy took over the questioning. And his hair and fingernails neatly cut, his clothes sweaty but superior and smart, the estate owner's voice was firm but smooth. "Justin, why is your name on this message to me?"

Ajeemah shook his head. His reply was firm. "Me dohn know, Massa. Me dohn know who send message."

"No favors asked of you? Nobody wants you to give him or sell him leather?"

"No, Massa."

"Nobody wants you to give or sell anything from another workshop?"

"No, Massa."

"Have you been talking to anybody—anybody different or anybody at all—about any kind of business or matter or anything?"

"Well—yes, Massa. I did want a cow."

"A cow? A cow for yourself?"

"Yes, Massa."

"And what happened?"

"I have talk with Mercury fo' cow."

"Ah! Mercury?"

"Yes, Massa."

"And what happened?"

"I did hear Mercury sell cow. So I ask Mercury sell me one cow."

"You wanted a cow for yourself?"

"Yes, Massa."

"And what did Mercury say?"

"Him say, 'cos me a slave, I first get permission from estate."

"Did you ask anybody for that permission?"

"No, Massa."

"Why not?"

"Too much bother, Massa."

"I see. Well, when you talked to Mercury, who else was there?"

"Who else?"

"Yes, who else was there?"

"Nobody else, Massa."

"Nobody else was there?"

"No, Massa. Nobody else."

"When did you talk to Mercury?"

"Three or four days past."

"Justin?"

"Yes, Massa."

"You must tell me the truth. You understand that?"

"Yes, Massa."

"This officer here will go and talk to Mercury. He will go and see if what you say is true. Telling lies won't help."

"No, Massa. Lies no good."

"If what Mercury says is different from what you say, you'll be in trouble. Bad trouble! For telling lies! You well understand?"

"Yes, Massa. Me know that."

"You still have a chance to tell me the truth."

"Is truth I tell, Massa. I tell all truth me know."

"You are not concealing anything you must and should tell me?"

"Me concealing nothing me must tell you, Massa. Nothing."

"All right. Go on back to work."

Ajeemah was shattered. All hope to escape was gone! He walked back to his workshop stunned, as if he'd been dealt a killing blow. He walked around lifeless, feeling like his heart cut down into the pit of his belly. His plan to escape was finished! Wiped out! Once the estate suspected you and all their powers landed on your trail, your plan and you yourself were doomed. Done for!

Right away Ajeemah suspected Kaleb. With all of his crying "sore back," with sharp talk, Kaleb had impressed him as only a poseur. Kaleb was like the general run of settled slave people. All beaten down, gutted and trampled, they didn't have the stomach for a fight. Yet Kaleb couldn't bring himself to expose the real planned gun attack on the estate, as he understood it. He merely spilled something enough to get the deadly hounds out, sniffing and stopping all plans for attack. What a good thing he and Mercury had thought of a watertight protection, for emergency, just in case. What a good thing they'd built in the cow-buying smokescreen, for both to stick to, if questioned. What a good thing, too, they decided to deny Kaleb as a third person present. Once the militia visited him, Mercury would cancel the order he gave him. He would cancel fighters, guns, horses, everything. Mercury understood everything. He would expect to be watched as he, Ajeemah, would be watched day and night.

Deeply disappointed, Ajeemah didn't know what else to do. Everything was hopeless. He became sadder and lonelier. Day after day and night after night, he went only to the leather workshop and to his log bed. He lost the feeling for his imaginary talks with his little son. It became too hard to feel that he saw Kufuo. And he stopped trying. He was full of rebellion he couldn't make work. He was hurt and sad. He was in agony that people could have so ganged up on him and abused him. So ganged up and spoiled his life that he had and wanted! So ganged up and made him a slave! He missed Africa. More than ever he missed his family; he missed his Africa and its way of life. Being a slave so reduced and spoiled a man! So took away all of your own life! So robbed all of you for another man called "Master"! So kept you as always an unfinished carcass for the lion's hunger! And a new longing stormed into Ajeemah.

He was wishing and wishing his people in Africa could read. He wished so much that at least his people could read and he could write and could send them a letter. Oh, he longed to make contact. But in that wishing, he knew he would live. He had to live. He had to damage the estate that so damaged him. He had to damage the estate and its owner—properly! Yet Ajeemah sank deeper into a sad, sorrowful feeling that wouldn't leave him. And he began muttering to himself as soon as he was alone.

In his own language, he mumbled to himself.

"Atu! Atu! My son, Atu! They changed my name. Have they changed your name, too? What day are you now born on, and what new name goes with the day? Oh, Atu, I would avenge us alone. But they are clever. They would make me waste the effort. They would let me waste myself for myself altogether. They would see I get no satisfaction for myself at all. But if I had you with me, Atu! If only I had you with me. We would avenge ourselves together. We would make this place a roaring fire, on every side. A roaring, roaring fire everywhere! And die in it, fighting! Fighting! Fighting! Oh, Atu! Atu! My son, Atu!"

Ajeemah didn't understand estate security. He didn't know the many ways the estate preserved itself safely. He didn't know that rebellion plotting, by a slave like him, was exactly why estates didn't have new slaves together who were related. Just as slaves of the same tribe were deliberately kept apart. And it worked. Keeping relatives and people of the same tribe apart, when new, prevented a lot of trouble. And so poor Ajeemah had no idea that his son Atu was fairly nearby—only twenty miles away on the Nelsons' estate. But, different from his sad and miserable father, Atu was going through his days all bouncy, good-natured, happy. He was full of an expectation, full of that fantastic moment he expected to happen.

He would get away. He'd prepared it. He'd set up his secret plan. Any day now would be his breakaway day—then, away! Good-bye to the Nelsons' estate, forever! Off and Sisi here I come!

Truly, though, Atu was now a different person from the young man he had been. With the life he lived, and being older, he had changed. He'd found himself standing up to punishments for troubles he had caused. He had become more muscular, tougher, and even heartless, cruel and sly. But he knew in every way he felt as he always had for Sisi.

Yet the testing times he'd gone through had really marked him. He'd gone through being cautioned twice, for stirring up trouble among his field workers. On three occasions he'd received lashes for slacking at work in his gang and encouraging others to do so too. He'd gone through a terrible flogging for being ringleader of a dispute, and for threatening behavior to his gang driver and to the headman. Atu had come to be known as a trouble-maker. Yet whenever he wanted, he could be the leading worker of his cane-field gang. He could put on his estate-pleasing act, though usually to conceal something he'd done.

When Atu's worst troubles had accumulated, about three years ago, he had stolen a gun. In his great moment of triumph—in his worship of the gun in his hand—Atu discovered the gun had no cartridges in it. And what a really bitter disappointment that was for Atu! But he kept the gun hidden. His desperation to get cartridges mounted. He searched, watched, waited. Searching the head-man's house to steal cartridges, he'd twice come near being caught. In fact, once, though he was not caught in the house, his movements had come un-der critical suspicion. He'd been up to something! Something! What was it? Only the well-organized and clever liar Atu had become had enabled him to talk his way out of that one. Atu *had* to be involved in a secret plan of action. So he still tried, planned again and watched and waited for the opportunity to steal cartridges. His strong obsessive feelings drove him on.

At last Atu was surprised to see that the estate had made him into a man he had never thought he'd ever be. Considering it, Atu saw that the estate had done everything to him to make him feel, know and become the worst of himself. And he felt full of wanting to throw everything back into the face of the estate. Atu had actually jumped for joy at the reason that spurred and drove him on to get cartridges for his gun. He whispered, "I must make them feel something from me. *Feel!* Feel *even* a little mashed up. For the big way they make *me* feel mashed up!"

All excited, Atu had jumped out of bed. In darkness in his hut room, he'd tossed his arms about and whispered angrily. "Spoil them! I going spoil them like them spoil me! Spoil them like hell! Damage them like vegetable pig half eat!" Atu punched the darkness. "Blast them—that Mr. and Mrs. Nelson!" He punched the darkness. "Blast them—that busherman the headman and that damn gang driver! Even that field cook woman who cuss me, call me 'uncivilize new African.' Blast them! Every one into piece-piece! Piece-piece! Like vegetable pig bite.up an' half eat!" Atu had walked about in the darkness, elated with his ideas about his dramatic shoot-up at the Nelson estate. "Oh, I going walk plenty middlenight. I going walk plenty middlenight. I mus' get cartridge! A little bagful. Oh, a little bagful will do!"

And Atu was kept going. Everything in him made him feel he now had a goal for himself. Everything in him made him feel and know he couldn't face the estate anymore without that goal. Something he himself worked out and wanted to do. All for himself! He couldn't get out of bed at sunrise to go and sweat in the sun till sundown for nothing. He couldn't dig seed-cane holes, weed cane fields, reap ripe cane, load wagons, roll barrels of sugar and rum onto wagons. He couldn't lift this, lift that. Couldn't yes, sir! yes, sir! yes, Massa! yes, Massa! and rush here and rush there. He couldn't take the whip lashes, take all the subjection for respect with none coming back to him, without a

goal of his own. He couldn't face anything more—
couldn't live at all—without knowing he would
stage a dramatic shoot-up of all the Nelson estate's
top people. And, he knew, eventually he would get
cartridges and another gun. Occupied like this, for
himself—waiting, watching, scheming, planning—
Atu managed to go to work. Atu avoided having to
be flogged out of bed to go to work. Then—all
unexpectedly—something else switched Atu on to
his present plan. And this same thing made Atu
wait three years for it to work. Three long years—
till now!

Atu bought a young baby horse cheaply: Its
mother had died. He bought the long-legged and
shaky two-week-old bay horse at Sunday market
from a man who'd bought himself out of slavery—a
freedman. Like other slaves, Atu had been allowed
his plot of land to grow food for his keep. Allowed
also to come to Sunday market to sell vegetables
and buy other food, slaves sometimes made and
saved enough money to buy themselves free. Atu
was totally taken up with this little horse. He even
managed to persuade the freedman to take him and

his horse home in his mule cart.

Right away, at the back of his hut, Atu began laughing and talking to the wobbly little horse like a long-lost friend. He hugged it. He looked into its eyes and said "Hullo!" He held his mouth up to its ear and whispered, "Adohfo! Adohfo!" He looked into its face. "D'you know meaning of Adohfo?" The big eyes of the little horse looked blank and sad. "So," Atu said, "you noh know, eh! I tell you. Adohfo is warrior! Warrior! You small now. But you will be big warrior. You born in Jamaica. Noh hard fo' you to know Jamaica. I noh born in Jamaica an' is hard fo' me to know Jamaica. I born in Africa. An' I know Africa! One day, Adohfo—warrior!— you take me to find ship, somehow, to take me back to Africa. We agree? . . . Good!" And Atu hugged Adohfo. "I mus' stow away on ship!"

Atu bought, begged and stole milk to feed Adohfo with a wooden spoon, till it supped the milk from a pán. He stole corn, which he pounded to feed his horse. Atu got up at five thirty every morning to have time to cut grass and get water to leave for his tethered colt. And the animal became the one real friend and companion in Atu's life.

Happiest time now for Atu since he left Africa! Wherever he was, a song memory of Sisi poured off the tip of his tongue. Waking up or going to bed, working in his field gang or walking through the village of huts, getting feed for the horse or feeding him, Atu hummed, whistled or sang:

> *Come here O*
> *Come let's play and dance osibi*
> *Come O Sisi . . .*

or:

> *Dugu-dugu-dom, dugu-dugu-dom, dugu-dugu-*
> *dom . . .*

Because of Adohfo, coming back to his hut every day was a happy event for Atu. Glad to see him too, the horse gave a gently low-pitched neigh like a chuckle. And once untethered, he followed Atu about the yard and stood beside him, anywhere.

Atu had his colt gelded. And how the horse swelled out in body and put on height astonished Atu. His Adohfo actually became a real full-size reddish-brown grown-up horse! Not able to believe it, Atu would look at the horse and shake his head. Such a picture of a fellow! His mane and tail were a joy to Atu to comb. His body was a pleasure to brush down.

Adohfo allowed Atu to ride him as if he took it as extended fun. But, being cautious, Atu didn't ride the horse to Sunday market; he just didn't want to show off Adohfo too much. For both practice and pleasure he rode his horse discreetly. Riding bareback, at night, or in dusky early morning, he regularly ventured from his dirt track onto the firmer surface of the main road.

Needless to say, Atu's planned escape was now his whole dream world. The reckless thumping of his heart all the time now reminded him his way was clear, his plan firm. His time on the Nelsons' estate was up! That very next Sunday morning, between three and four A.M., he would disappear on Adohfo's back like wind! For good! Oh, for good! Never ever to return! And no heading for the nearest port, either, where he might be traced. No heading for anywhere other than the city port.

There, he would find a way to hide. He would hide till he found a ship to stow away on. Whatever should happen—no coming back!

On this his last evening in from his slave work, Atu had to hold on to himself. This dangerous and secret excitement was too much. A pressure inside him made him feel his heart could burst. He had to walk about to slow down and keep a grip on himself.

In the dusky daylight of Saturday evening Atu gave Adohfo a good last feed. He stood stroking Adohfo, talking to him. The estate overseer and headman rode up to his hut and came straight around to the back where Atu was feeding his horse.

"Simon," the overseer said, as they had renamed Atu, "we've come to take the horse."

At first, for Atu, everything was unreal like a dream. His face became a blank. Then, almost slowly, Atu's eyes and whole face became a total alarm. "Me horse?" he said. "Me Adohfo?"

"What you thought was your horse," the overseer said calmly.

"Sir. Is fo' me, this horse!" Atu stressed with his five years of plantation English. "Is fo' me, this horse! Me buy him, cheap-cheap. All of whole two years' money go on him, sir. What me save from me food I grow in me garden, sir. Me buy him cheap-cheap. Me buy him from a baby horse half dead. Me look after him, look after him, till now him big. Big-big, sir!"

The overseer spoke icily. "A slave isn't allowed to keep a horse. And Simon, you should know that."

Atu shook his head. His helpless arms waved. His whole body shook in desperation. "Sir. Nobody tell me noh keep a horse. Nobody tell me!"

"We don't know you're going to break the rules till you break them."

"Sir. Big busherman, sir. This me horse, me horse, everything, everything, fo' me I have!"

"You never really had it, Simon. That's what I'm telling you."

"Massa busher, me own money, sir. Me own money buy the horse, a baby half dead. Me very own-a own-a money, sir!"

"Simon, you yourself belong to the estate. The grass you feed the horse on is estate grass. The time you used to look after the horse belonged to the estate. Just as you are estate property, the horse is estate property."

"Sir. Me look after me horse every day before worktime an' after worktime. Mostly in dusk an' darkness."

"That was only estate rest time that you used. That was time for you to rest for work next day. It wasn't your time." The overseer looked at the headman and nodded.

The two men left the yard. The headman led Adohfo behind the horse he rode. Atu followed. He stopped. Atu was all disbelief, all pain. He stood watching his horse disappear in the dusk of early night, passing the tropical trees.

Atu felt he had lost all speech. As if an explosion had deafened and dazed him, his head was a fuzzy confusion. He felt he couldn't move. Yet his legs took him walking up and down the dusty village road till he went to bed.

Deep and sullen in his work gang next day, Atu

didn't speak to anybody. On the following day, to his absolute astonishment, Atu looked up from his work and saw the headman sitting on the back of his Adohfo! The headman had ridden up; he talked to the gang driver. Atu stood stunned like a statue with an instrument in his hand. Atu had never seen his horse saddled and in a bridle with bit and reins. Adohfo was spectacular! Atu thought. Spectacular! And *him* is the rider! Fixed intensely, watching the horse and rider, Atu whispered, "Adohfo! Oh! Oh, Adohfo!" He looked away in deep thought. And Atu continued working.

Next morning, Adohfo was found in the stable lying awkwardly on his side. The horse was in miserable pain. His two front legs were broken. With much alarm and rush-about, soon Adohfo was shot, ending his pain.

Mr. Nelson roared a field marshal's authority at Atu. "Simon! What d'you know about the injured horse? Did you commit that savagery? Did you break his legs?"

Atu was calm, fatally calm. "Yes, Massa. Is me do it. Me do it, Massa."

"And what makes you think you could get away with it? Eh?"

"I dohn look to get away with it, Massa. Me dohn see it so."

"You had better not see it so. You are going to be punished!"

"Yes, Massa. Me know that. Me know that, Massa."

All the estate slave people were brought together in the work yard. An audience of well over three hundred! And the people were to watch as Atu was flogged and flogged severely.

On the fourth day after Atu lost his horse another sad scene followed. Atu's body was found sprawling across the Great House gateway. Mr. and Mrs. Nelson had driven up in their carriage at two A.M. from a function in the town. As usual, the driver stopped and climbed down to open the gate. And there was Atu, dressed as he was after his flogging, in his field clothes.

Mrs. Nelson stayed in the carriage. Mr. Nelson came out and looked at Atu, most crossly. "How dare he do a thing like this here! Who told him he could do this here? The disrespect of it. The audacity! . . . Pull out the long knife from his chest! No, drag him out of the way till daylight." And he settled in the carriage again, finally saying, "Made more trouble than he was worth." But as he remembered standing over Atu being severely flogged, he whispered, "Poor devil!"

Then, there was a strange happening. And nobody could explain it. At the exact moment Atu's lowered body touched the bottom of his grave, his father Ajeemah had an unusual experience. With a saddle in his hand for repair, Ajeemah gave a dreadfully pained cry—and fell backward. He held himself stricken, as if suddenly wounded. "Me son! Me Kufuo! Shark eat him up. Shark nyam him! I see him a-swim. I see him a-swim 'pon big sea. A-come to me. An' shark grab him. Oh, shark grab me Kufuo! An' shark eat him up."

Felix was not totally surprised, but concerned. He tried to comfort Ajeemah. "Never mind," he said. "Never mind. Wha's really the matter? You in pain? Where it hurt? Where?"

"I dohn know," Ajeemah said. "I dohn know. Me

see like a vision. I see little Kufuo, a-swim, a-swim, 'pon the ocean, an' shark grab him."

"How you feel?" Felix asked. "How you feel?"

"No good. No good."

Felix saw to it that Ajeemah was taken to the estate hospital. News went around the estate that the leatherman African had gone mad. That same evening Bella, a Great House servant, went to see Ajeemah.

"Who say you to come see me?" Ajeemah asked Bella.

"Nobody. I miself wahn come. I get permission. So I come."

Ajeemah had seen this long-legged Bella about occasionally. She always had a superiority beyond everybody else. He looked at her with doubts. "Why you come see me?"

"What you mean, why? You's a person. An' not well."

"You did hear militiaman come question me?"

"Everybody did hear redcoat man come question you."

"What people say, when them hear so?"

"You's a fairly new African. But not everybody suspicious."

"Suspicious me do something bad?"

"Yeahs."

"You did suspicious of me?"

"Well—tell the truth, I did pick up the note 'bout you, at Great House. An' gave it to Massa."

"You did pick up the note?"

"Yeahs."

"You see me name on it an' give it up?"

"Me didn't see you name."

"Didn't see it?"

"No. Me cahn read, you know."

"You born Jamaica. Live at Great House. An' cahn read?"

"Yes," Bella said. "True."

"We must get practice quick-quick. Me must know to read an' write."

"You?"

"Yes, me."

"Good-good ambition. Plenty-plenty of we would like to read an' write."

"Backra people wohn let it. Wohn let it. Them

will say, Nayga wohn work 'pon estate when them can read."

"Backra people dohn have to have *all* the say *all* the time. Like you, I going learn reading."

"You born here. An' still wha' happen is wha' you do fo' them."

"Justin? Everybody know you is a skill man. An' plenty-plenty people think you make you life too, too selfish."

"Me? A man who selfish."

"Well—I miself—I think you keep youself too much to youself. An' really, you not going back to Africa. You not going back, you know."

Ajeemah was alarmed. "Me? Noh going back?"

"Yes, Justin. You not going back."

"Me live in Jamaica fo' all me days to come?"

"Yes. One day we all, all get freedom."

"Freedom I use to go home. Back to Africa."

"You won't. No Nayga in Jamaica go back to Africa. Nobody go."

Bella's words sank into Ajeemah like a command, a revelation, a truth, but also an accusation. Though he knew nobody who went back, her words would find no acceptance in him. He was firm. "This land—this land—no, no burial place fo' me."

"Plenty African bury here. Plenty. But fo' you, Justin, before that day come, plenty-plenty can happen fo' you."

He looked at Bella with a gaze that was strong and long. Something between a man and a woman had clicked. And her face, her body, her whole presence sent a warm happiness through him. In a quieter voice Bella said, "I bring you a piece a Great House cake. An' some milk with honey."

Ajeemah and Bella became great friends. Knowing Bella changed Ajeemah drastically.

Bella was ambitious. She longed to get her freedom and get her own home and land. She could not persuade Ajeemah they should both buy their freedom. Ajeemah was absolutely against ever paying anybody for his freedom. But once he felt and began to enjoy a wonderful new sense of partnership with Bella, he too desperately wanted to secure a way to get his own land. Bella was a long-established servant at the Great House. As such she enjoyed a special status. She began to use her influence to win ways to get land, when they were able to buy. She encouraged Ajeemah to begin making sandals and shoes to sell. Ajeemah also began to increase his food growing on his garden plot of land. And this friendship with Bella encouraged him to make his takings at Sunday market show an increase.

Ajeemah and Bella were married thirteen years after he arrived in Jamaica. He was then forty-nine years old. One year later he and Bella had a baby daughter. The day the girl child arrived on was practically unbelievable. The child was exactly another Sunday-born child, as Atu's lamented Sisi was. Surely, the voice of fate and destiny was clear and eloquent! Surely, a hidden mystery pointed a finger where something special should happen! Naturally, Bella and Ajeemah gave their baby girl the name Sisi. And slow-paced change kept on arriving into Ajeemah's life.

Slave owners didn't want the proposed law to end slavery ever to get passed. But with all their terrible attacks on it, their bitter rages and planned resistances against it, the slavery-abolition law was passed victoriously. But for loss of property, the ex-owners in the British West Indies received twenty million pounds from the British government. And Mr. Fairworthy and Mr. Nelson took their handsome share. Yet it seemed the ex-owners would stay angry and bitter forever, never able to acknowledge the people's lives they had dispossessed and lived on. Essentially now, though, freedom—freedom!—had come for Ajeemah, like all the other slaves. And here he was, numbered in with the last generation of people who emptied their work lives into other people's bank accounts. Here he was, in with those whose two-hundred-year bondage in the West Indies had ended.

Now an unbelievable first day was coming. Ajeemah and Bella, with the other estate slave people, waited up all night to welcome their first day of freedom. They waited and greeted the dawn with singing and joyful prayers of thanksgiving. They cheered and sang till dawn became the broad daylight of August 1, 1838, and open celebrations could begin. Singing both jubilant and sad songs, the ex-slave people collected together, and, slowly together, they moved away from the estate.

Some of the former slaves went and joined the few established free people. Others began putting together their own new villages.

At nineteen years old, in 1840, Sisi was married. In a white bridal gown, on the arm of Julius, son of Quaco-Sam and Phibba, she left their church ceremony. They came to her parents' home, a very crowded place. People were still intoxicated with their newfound freedom, setting up homes, and getting land, and learning to be free citizens. Ajeemah had opened a shoemaking and repair business in their new village. Bella had become the village seamstress. And a wedding reception at their home on this gloriously sunny afternoon was a specially happy occasion.

Ajeemah's suit material had come from England. He dressed like a wealthy estate owner. Beginning his speech, Ajeemah welcomed everybody. He went on and said, "I'm now sixty-nine years old. I was taken from my motherland, Africa, thirty-three years ago. Plenty things happened since then.

Plenty-plenty! But first best thing for me was that special day when I went mad. An' a person I'd only seen going about came to see me, to nurse me, with cake, an' milk an' honey. What a wonderful day, when in my madness I looked in Bella's eyes, an' I saw love! Such a lonely man I was! I tell you, I never forget my family in Africa. Sometimes, fo' them I shed a quiet tear. But I've made such big treasure chests of new memories. Through Bella! And Sisi. And all good friends here. With Julius now added.

"Fo' thirty-three years I kept something special. Very special! That something was a bride-gift I carried in my sandals as a joke to present to the parents of Sisi, the girl my son Atu was to marry. An', going, we were captured. Kidnapped and brought here. Well—by some freak of providence I managed to hide, keep an' protect that gift, to travel with it, an' keep it here in Jamaica. An' fo' thirty-three years I keep it!" And taking the two thick plates of gold sheets, one from each pocket, and holding them up in his hands, Ajeemah went on. "I present this eventful African bride-gift to this Jamaican Sisi and husband Julius."

Ajeemah was cheered and cheered. He went on. "I tell you, this new husband an' wife stay here with Bella an' me for a while. But I did get value of this old gift. I hear this gold will buy them own land, an' own house."

The people could not contain themselves. Everybody wanted to see this amazing surprise of gold, kept secret for so long. The wedding people pressed forward. Some people took the gold from hand to hand and weighed it up and down, groaning astonishment. Some simply touched it, feeling the cold metal. Others merely looked on, as if they saw relics from an ancient Egyptian tomb, and kept their distance.

Then the people stood, looking at Ajeemah. They didn't seem to know what to do, how to love him and honor him, for his depth of endurance and personal loyalty to his past. Obviously overcome by the moment, Ajeemah merely stood there. Somebody began to clap. And everybody clapped.

It seemed the handclapping would never stop. In the endless hand-burning applause, Sisi began to cry. She had known nothing of the gold. She had known little of her father's painful story. The occasion overwhelmed her and made her ache with an agony of happiness, but also with other mixed-in feelings that racked her with distress. She felt a guilt and a shame. Her father was so strong! So strong! What he believed in and did were of great substance and depth! And her values were so, so shallow! Yet she preferred hers. She did not like the name Sisi. It sounded too African. And she couldn't help it. Nothing African was popular. She endured the name only because it meant so much to her father. Most people called her Emma. And that was the name she liked. It was the name Emma she liked and wanted and would say her name was. And she would never tell her father. And because of Julius, and her mother's love, and her father's suffering and strength and his amazing surprise gift of gold, and all the people here on such a big, overwhelming day, she wept. And—in spite of all the caring and comforting of the women—she cried on and on.